SCOOBY-DOO! and YOU:

A Collect the Clues Mystery

THE CASE OF THE HAUNTED HOUND

By Vicki Erwin

SCHOLASTIC INC.

New York Toronto London Auckland Sydney
Mexico City New Delhi Hong Kong

ISBN 0-439-21755-5

12 11 10   4 5/0

Cover and interior illustrations by Duendes del Sur
Cover and interior design by Madalina Stefan

Printed in the U.S.A.

First Scholastic printing, November 2000

For my son, Bryan

"**W**e're over here!" Fred calls to you as you step inside Woofie's Hot Dogs. "There's plenty of room."

You join the Scooby gang in a big corner booth, squeezing in on the end beside Fred.

The waitress arrives at almost the same moment you do, carrying the longest hot dog you've ever seen.

"Like, I don't want to be a bother, but I asked for two foot-long dogs not one two-foot long one," Shaggy says, licking his lips.

The waitress apologizes and turns away.

1

Shaggy grabs her arm. "No sense in wasting that. We'll snack on it while we're waiting for our foot-longs."

The waitress smiles and sets the long hot dog between Scoob and Shag.

"Race you to the middle," Shaggy challenges. He picks up the hot dog and Scooby opens his mouth.

"Like, wait!" Shaggy drowns the hot dog in catsup, mustard, relish, and onions. "Go!" They gobble from opposite ends of the dog, ending nose to nose.

"Groovy," says Shaggy, rubbing his stomach.

Scooby rubs his stomach, too, as he nods.

"That's another doggy problem solved," says Velma with a laugh. She turns to you. "We just finished tying up the loose ends of a mystery we call the Haunted Hound."

You lean forward, wanting to hear more.

Fred pulls out a blue notebook and sets it on the table in front of you. "This time it was my turn to write down what happened in our mystery," he says.

"And that's only right since we got involved when Fred won a mystery writing contest," Daphne explains.

"The prize was a weekend at a bed and breakfast. Wish you could have been there to help us. But it's not too late — you can still try your hand at figuring out what happened," Velma says. "If you want."

You nod eagerly.

Fred flips open the notebook. "Here are a few hints to help you. If you see 👁 👁, that means you've met a suspect. And if you see  then it's a clue."

"And, when you finish reading, we'll talk about what happened. Sometimes that helps make sense of everything. We always talk over the clues before we solve a mystery." Daphne smiles.

"Do you have your Clue Keeper with you?" Fred asks.

You stick your hand in your jacket pocket to check. It's there. You pull it out and set it on the table. Then you open Fred's Clue Keeper and begin to read.

Clue Keeper Entry 1

"Here we are, gang," I announced as I parked the Mystery Machine in front of a large stone mansion. A small sign hung on the door. It said THE HAUNTED HOUND.

"Like, this is the biggest pad I've ever seen!" Shaggy said as he climbed out of the van.

"It's beautiful," Daphne agreed.

"Don't you love those towers?" asked

Velma, pointing to the two towers on either end of the house.

"Not if they're really haunted," Shaggy said with a gulp. "They would make a perfect pad for a ghost." Scooby nodded.

Velma, Daphne, and I laughed. "It's just the name that sounds creepy," I said, going to the back of the van to unload our bags. "It's really just a cool bed and breakfast. You know, an inn."

A tall thin woman with long dark hair opened the wooden front door. "Fred?" she asked.

"I'm Fred." I dropped the duffel bag I was pulling out of the van and walked up to meet her.

"I'm Cathy Jaffe, your hostess." She held out a hand and we shook. "Congratulations on winning our contest. There were many, many entries, but your solution to the mystery was very clever."

I'd entered a mystery writing contest in the back of a magazine and my prize was a weekend at the Haunted Hound. "It's not that hard when you've solved as many mysteries as we have," I replied.

"You mean you're truly detectives?" Ms. Jaffe glanced over my shoulder at the gang.

"We like a good mystery now and then," Velma said. "Why?"

"Then you don't scare easily?" Ms. Jaffe asked hopefully.

"It depends on what you're talking about," Daphne said.

"And which one of us you're talking to," Shaggy added.

"I bought this place shortly after the owner died. Do you know who used to live here?" asked Ms. Jaffe.

"Neil Warnicke, the famous mystery writer," I said. "At least that's what your letter said."

"That's right. You probably also know that Mr. Warnicke based his main character, a dog, on his Jack Russell terrier. He always said that Perry was his best friend, the only friend he would trust his secrets to," Ms. Jaffe said.

"*A rog?*" said Scooby, his ears perking up.

"Now you've got Scooby's attention," said Velma, smiling.

I was starting to get the feeling from Ms. Jaffe that something wasn't quite right at the Haunted Hound. "And you think that maybe Mr. Warnicke had some secrets?" I asked.

"I'm almost certain he did," Ms. Jaffe said. "When he died, his niece expected to inherit his fortune." She paused.

"But?" I asked to encourage her to go on.

"There was no fortune to be found!"

"So his secret was that he spent all his money?" Velma asked.

"No one believes that. His niece thinks that he hid it. He had a history of playing games," said Ms. Jaffe. "But it's not Mr. Warnicke or his niece I'm worried about. It's the dog."

"Isn't the dog dead?" asked Daphne. "I thought I read that he died the same day Mr. Warnicke did."

Scooby sniffed sadly.

"Yes, but I think if there is a secret, the

dog's ghost may still be trying to guard it," Ms. Jaffe said.

Shaggy grabbed the duffel bags and threw them back in the van. He and Scooby jumped into the back seat. "Like, let's get out of here before that haunted hound shows up!" Shaggy shouted.

"We're not leaving," I answered.

"What makes you think there's a ghost dog?" Velma asked Ms. Jaffe.

"I've been working on the house for a few months now and there are things," — she swallowed hard — "noises, that scare me. I've heard a dog walking across the floor of the attic in the middle of the night — his nails click, click, clicking on the bare boards. But even worse is the howling!"

Shag and Scoob ran back to the Mystery Machine and disappeared under a blanket we had in the back seat.

Ms. Jaffe's voice dropped to a whisper. "I think the dog is protecting whatever it is that Mr. Warnicke hid in the house."

Before any of us could say anything, a

small red convertible roared up the driveway and screeched to a halt in front of the Mystery Machine.

"Cathy! You're finally open!" A red-haired girl  climbed out of the car without

opening the door. "I hope you've reserved my old room. You promised I could come for the grand opening!"

"Hi, Sally," Ms. Jaffe said in a flat voice. "This weekend is by invitation only. But I'd love to have you come next weekend when we open for business."

The young woman's lips began to quiver and tears welled up in her eyes. "I miss Uncle Neil so much. If I could just come inside the house where we had so many wonderful times, I'd feel so much better." She dabbed at her eyes with a tissue she had pulled out of her pocket.

Ms. Jaffe sighed.

"You won't even know I'm around and I'll leave before you and . . ." She peeked around the corner of her tissue at me. "Your guests start the celebration." Sally sniffed a few times.

"Don't worry," Ms. Jaffe said to the young woman. "We'll make room for you. Sally Warnicke, I'd like you to meet Fred, the winner of the Neil Warnicke Mystery Contest."

"You're a writer?" Sally's sobs quieted and she removed the tissue. "Me, too."

"I try," I said modestly. "These are my friends, Daphne and Velma. And over by the van, that's Scooby-Doo and Shaggy."

Scoob and Shag lifted their heads and waved.

"Sally is Neil Warnicke's niece, in case you haven't figured that out," Ms. Jaffe said. "Come inside and I'll show you to your rooms. There are two more guests staying here this weekend."

"If you saw the 👀 on page 10, you know that we already have a suspect. Answer the following questions in your Clue Keeper."

1. What is the suspect's name?

2. What does she do for a living?

3. Why is she interested in The Haunted Hound?

13

Clue Keeper Entry 2

Scooby and Shaggy finally left the van. After everyone gathered their luggage, we followed Ms. Jaffe into the house. I felt like I should help Sally Warnicke with her bag, it was almost as big as she was. "I can handle it," she said when I offered, and she dragged the big suitcase through the front door.

Inside, the door creaked slowly closed and we were in a large round hallway with a

14

winding staircase on one side and a set of closed doors on the other. A curved archway led to the back of the house.

"Your rooms are on the second floor," said Ms. Jaffe. "And Sally, you can have the north tower. It still needs another coat of paint, but since you insist on staying . . ."

"That will be perfect," Sally said quickly. "And I love what you've done to this place."

I'm no interior decorator, but with the dark wood walls and the only light coming from a small leaded window halfway up the stairs and light bulbs set into holders in the wall, I couldn't imagine what improvements Ms. Jaffe had made. It did make me wonder what it must have been like before.

The doors to one side opened a crack and a very short, very round woman stepped out, then shut the doors firmly behind her. She wore a business suit and high heels. "I thought I heard voices," she said in a deep, whispery voice. She put one finger over her lips. "Shh, Trent is trying to work and the sooner he finishes, the sooner we'll be out of your hair."

Ms. Jaffe ran her hand over her hair, pushing it away from her face. "Margy, you promised you'd be finished this weekend. As it is, I've had to delay the opening twice so Trent won't be disturbed."

"You know how important this book is to my company and to Trent," Margy said, her face reddening. "With Neil gone and the manuscript to his final book missing, we need his book. Our customers are expecting it."

"Margy, darling, it's so good to see you." Sally stepped forward and kissed the shorter woman on each cheek.

"Sally?" Margy stepped away from Neil Warnicke's niece, her eyes growing large. "Why . . . why aren't you home working on your book?"

"And why is Trent Kendall working in my uncle's study? What is he working on?" Sally asked.

Ms. Jaffe stepped between the two women. "Margy, Sally, I'm trying to run a business here. And if the two of you can't get along for one day, you will have to leave. Margy Shaw, I'd like you to meet Fred, the young man I was telling you about."

Ms. Shaw stepped around Sally and looked me up and down. I felt like a display in a museum! "Hmmm," she said. "You wrote the solution to Cathy's little story, did you?"

"Yes, ma'am, I did," I said.

"Good job, young man, good job. You keep writing and someday Mystery Books Ink may publish one of your books. I'm the editor in chief and I'm on the lookout for someone to take Neil Warnicke's place on the bestseller list. Looks like you're a dog lover, too." She patted Scooby Doo on the head. "This one could maybe be a detective."

"He's already helped solve a few mysteries," Velma said.

"But Margy, I thought I was going to be your next star," Sally said, pouting.

"You'd be my star if you could find that

blasted manuscript your uncle said he was working on. I'd let you finish it and even put your name on the cover," said Margy. "It must be here somewhere," she added almost in a whisper.

"I plan to write a book better than anything Uncle Neil ever did," Sally said as she started climbing the stairs, dragging her heavy bag behind her. I reached for the bag again to help her carry it, but Sally pushed me away without saying a word. I let her go.

"Ms. Shaw, do you publish any cookbooks?" Shaggy asked. We heard his stomach rumble, echoed by Scooby's stomach.

"Oh, my! Food! You must think I'm a horrible hostess," Ms. Jaffe said. "I plan on serving a bedtime snack in the library as soon as you've unpacked."

"That would be super, Ms. Jaffe," Daphne said. "We'd all like a chance to freshen up."

Shaggy sighed. "I guess I could wait a little longer."

"Did you see the 👁 👁 on page 15? That means you've found suspect number two. Write the answers to the following questions in your Clue Keeper."

1. What is the suspect's name?

2. What does she do for a living?

3. Why is she interested in Neil Warnicke's house?

Clue Keeper Entry 3

The doors on our left burst open and a man stood in the middle of the doorway, his hands on his hips . "Quiet! I must insist upon quiet!" he said.

He had a dark mustache with streaks of gray in it, but he was bald.

He wore a shirt and black pants, but no shoes or socks.

"Trent, I'm so sorry." Ms. Shaw hurried to his side. "Everyone is going upstairs to their rooms right away."

"They are staying here? No guests, I said, no GUESTS!" His voice grew louder and louder until he was shouting.

"Trent! You mustn't make Fred and his friends feel unwelcome," Ms. Jaffe said. "Fred, Velma, Daphne, Shaggy, and Scooby, this is Trent Kendall."

"Pleased to meet you," I said, holding out my hand.

Mr. Kendall looked at it but didn't make any move to shake.

I dropped it.

"Like, who's the Kendall dude?" Shaggy whispered to me.

Ms. Shaw heard him.

"I'm sure you must have read some of the books Mr. Kendall has written," she said.

"Then they'd be among the few," Mr. Kendall said gruffly.

"My work is too advanced for most people. But this biography I'm writing of Neil Warnicke could finally make me famous," he said. "If I only could find that lost manuscript and use it in my biography, everyone would want to read it."

He turned his back to us. "Coming Margy?" he asked as he marched back the way he'd come.

Ms. Shaw didn't follow after him.

"I apologize," Ms. Jaffe said, closing the doors behind him. "I purchased Mr. Warnicke's library as well as the house, and I'm letting Mr. Kendall use all of Mr. Warnicke's papers for research on a biography he's writing about Neil."

"Maybe this wasn't a good weekend for us to come," I said.

"We're not leaving before we eat," said Shaggy.

"Rood rirst," Scooby said.

"You're not leaving at all!" Ms. Jaffe insisted. "This is a big house. There's room for everyone! Follow me and I'll show you your rooms."

We picked up our luggage and followed Ms. Jaffe up the stone stairs.

"Like, did you see the cool on page 21? We're marking that bald-headed dude as a suspect. Write some more answers to these questions in your Clue Keeper."

1. What's the suspect's name?

2. What does he do for a living?

3. Why is he at The Haunted Hound?

25

Clue Keeper Entry 4

We climbed the stairs, higher and higher.

Behind me I heard Shaggy and Scooby panting. "How much farther?" Shaggy asked in a weak voice.

"We're here," said Ms. Jaffe as the stairs ended at a long, dark hallway. "I thought I'd put Fred in the Purple Pooch room." Ms. Jaffe pointed to a door at the end of the hall.

"Velma, you and Daphne can stay in the Dizzy Dog. Shaggy and Scooby, the Capital Canine is yours." We were in adjoining rooms, all named after books by Neil Warnicke.

"Bye," Ms. Shaw said, hurrying down the hall.

"I'm in the south tower room, if you need anything," Ms. Jaffe went on. "And Mr. Kendall and Ms. Shaw are staying in the other wing of the house. So you don't need to worry about making noise and bothering

Mr. Kendall. I'm going to invite them to join us for a nighttime snack, too."

"Meet you back here as soon as we unpack," said Daphne as she and Velma stepped into their Dizzy Dog room.

"Make it quick," said Shaggy, "or Scoob and I won't have the strength to find the kitchen."

"We'll make sure you get there," I said as I went into my room. It was as purple as the name. But the bed was big and there was a shelf of Neil Warnicke mysteries beside the bed. I picked out the *Case of the Purple Pooch* and laid it beside the bed to read later.

As I stepped out into the hall to meet the gang, thunder rolled and lightning flashed.

"I hope Ms. Jaffe wasn't planning on feeding us outdoors," Velma said.

"It looks like a big storm," Daphne said.

"Did you say storm?" Shaggy asked as it continued to thunder and lightning. "I hope it doesn't close the kitchen." He raced down the stairs with Scooby close behind him.

Ms. Jaffe was waiting at the bottom of the steps. Thunder boomed louder, rattling the windows. "I've laid out a snack in the library. I asked Sally to join us, but she decided to turn in early. Margy and Trent said they'd come by in a few minutes."

Mr. Warnicke's library was huge. In the center of the room there was a big table, covered with sandwiches, cookies, and decorated cakes. Shaggy and Scooby rushed past me and grabbed plates.

Shaggy took a cookie off Scooby's plate. "You have to eat your sandwiches first, then dessert," he said.

Scooby ate the tiny sandwiches on his plate in one gulp, then took the cookie back and ate it.

"Great chow," Shaggy mumbled between bites.

"I'm glad you boys are enjoying it," Ms. Jaffe said, thunder almost drowning out her words. "Oh, my. I'd better go get some candles — just in case. When the others join you, please pour them some tea, Daphne, will you?"

"Sure thing," Daphne said.

"Like, there's already a bunch of candles here," said Shaggy, wandering over to the mantle and pointing to a large golden candle holder with many candles.

"What a great candelabra," Daphne said, looking up at the candle holder. "Too bad it's got a chip at the base. It's still beautiful, though."

The lights flickered.

The sound of a dog's howl filled the room. Everyone looked at Scooby-Doo.

"*Rot re*," he said.

"It must have been a neighbor's dog," said Velma as the lights flickered again.

Then everything went dark.

"Yikes!" Shaggy shouted. "Scooby-Doo, where are you?"

"I'll light the candles," I said. I reached for the candelabra. Then I heard it — click, click, click.

"Sc-Sc-Scooby?" Shaggy said in a shaky voice.

"Grrrr," a dog growled.

I lit a match and in the flickering light we all saw it — a huge, Jack Russell terrier crouched in front of one of the bookshelves.

"Don't let him get the food," Shaggy said as he and Scooby huddled under the table.

The dog growled again.

A breeze came out of nowhere and blew out the candles I'd managed to light.

Thunder boomed, sounding like it was right over our heads and when lightning flashed again, the dog's eyes and teeth gleamed even brighter.

"Like, let's get out of here!" Shaggy and Scooby ran past me.

"Whoa!" Shaggy said. I heard the sound of a skid then a thud. "Noooooooo!" he yelled in the dark.

I heard footsteps on the stairs, then the lights came back on. When I looked behind me, the dog was gone. So were Shaggy and Scooby.

Clue Keeper Entry 5

"Scooby? Shaggy?" Velma called.

There was no answer.

"Where did they go?" Daphne asked.

"And where's the dog? You guys saw the dog, too, didn't you?" I asked.

"I did," said Velma, "but right now I'm more worried about our friends."

"Being so far out in the country, the electricity is so unreliable," Ms. Jaffe said, returning with several candles and holders. It continued to thunder and lightning.

"The dog — we saw it sitting over here," I said to Ms. Jaffe. I walked over to the shelf. There was some powder on the floor 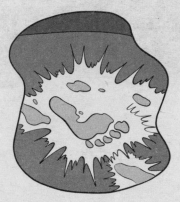 and I leaned down to look at it. "That's strange," I said as Velma and Daphne joined

me. I could make out a bare footprint — a human foot — in the powder.

Ms. Jaffe sat in a chair, her hands covering her face. "What am I going to do? I can't run a haunted bed and breakfast. No one will come."

"Did you happen to see Scooby and Shaggy?" asked Velma. "They were here when the lights went off, but they're gone now."

Ms. Shaw rushed into the room. She'd changed into jeans, a blue shirt, and cowboy boots. "Thank heaven the lights came back on. We came to see if you had any candles," Ms. Shaw said.

Mr. Kendall came in and headed straight toward me. His bare feet slapped the hard stone floor. "Get away from my *papers*!" he shouted, grabbing me by the shoulder and pulling me up.

"I wasn't bothering them," I said. "I was trying to figure out where the dog went."

"The dog?" Ms. Shaw turned pale.

"We saw a giant Jack Russell terrier when the lights went out," Daphne said. It thundered again, followed by lightning.

"But most of all we're worried about our friends, Shaggy and Scooby. They've disappeared," said Velma. She walked across the room. "Look at this. I think Shag and Scoob must have slid on this rug. Didn't it use to be over there?"

Ms. Jaffe nodded.

"I heard a thud," said Daphne.

The rug was heaped in front of a wall.

"It's time for us to have a look around, guys," said Velma.

"I think the rest of us should go to our rooms — with some candles just in case," said Ms. Jaffe. "Please let me know when you find your friends."

"And stay away from my papers," Mr. Kendall muttered as he followed Ms. Jaffe.

Ms. Shaw shrugged and her boots clattered as she left the room.

Fred's Mystery-Solving Tips

"Okay, we have a clue. Did you see the on page 34? The questions below will help you make sense of what the clue means."

1. What was the clue?

2. How do you think it got there?

3. Who could have left it?

Clue Keeper Entry 6

This is what Shaggy told me happened to him after the wall opened.

Shaggy felt his way through the darkness until he touched something warm and furry. "Is that you, Scoobs?"

"Reah," Scooby answered, his voice shaking.

"Where are we? Fred? Velma? Daphne?" Shaggy whispered.

"*Rit's rark,*" said Scooby.

"Like, I don't think we're in the library anymore." Shaggy felt along the wall. "And I don't even know how we got here. I slipped on the rug, ran into the wall, felt it open, and then everything was even darker than it was before."

"*Reah, re, roo,*" Scooby said.

"Wish we had some of those candles." Shaggy sighed. "Let's see if we can find a way out of here." Shaggy felt his way along the dark hallway, with Scooby hanging on to his neck. "Scooby, not so tight, man." Scoob loosened his grip, but didn't let go.

"Here's some steps. You want to try them?" Shaggy asked. Scooby shook his head.

Click, click, click — they heard the sound of a dog walking slowly and steadily behind them. Scooby pushed Shaggy out of the way and took the lead.

Grrrr! a growl filled the dark passageway. Shaggy gulped and reached out for

Scooby, grabbing his collar. "Wait a minute, pal," he said. "Let's chill for a minute. That wasn't you growling by any chance?"

The dog turned around and Shaggy found himself staring into the gleaming black eyes of a Jack Russell terrier. He yelled as the dog's mouth opened and its shiny teeth lit up the hallway.

"That sounded like Shaggy!" Velma cried.

We'd finished searching the first floor and had climbed to the second to try to find Scooby and Shaggy.

"And it sounds like it's coming from behind this wall!" said Daphne.

I knocked on the wall and it sounded hollow. "Shaggy! We're right here," I called.

"Help!" Shaggy yelled.

"*Relp!*" Scooby repeated.

I pushed, but nothing happened. I heard growling behind the wall, followed by pounding.

Velma and Daphne ran their hands along the wall, searching for a sign of an opening, then the panel opened and Scooby and Shaggy

fell on top of us. I caught a glimpse of the ghost dog running up some stairs as the panel slid back as quickly as it had slid opened.

Shaggy and Scooby stayed in a heap on the floor, holding on to each other.

"You fellas all right?" Velma asked.

"I think so," said Shaggy, "but someone needs to call the dog catcher."

"Looks like you guys found a secret passage," I said, still trying to figure out how to make the door slide open when I wanted it to.

"I think it opened when I pressed this," said Velma. She pressed a plaster flower that looked like a decoration. And she was right, the door slid open.

"Don't go in there!" Shaggy warned. "There's a monster dog waiting for a snack."

"We do need a flashlight or some candles. It's too dark to see anything," I said.

"Except for that shiny powder again," said Velma.

"And Fred, it looks like some got on your shirt ⚬━⚬," said Daphne, brushing my shoulders.

I tried to see, but it was on the back of my shirt.

"It shines like the dog's eyes and teeth," said Daphne.

At that, Shaggy and Scooby ran into their room and slammed the door.

"Like, I wish we'd had a flashlight when we found that secret passage. But, you should have found the on page 42. So what do you make of this clue?"

on page 42.

1. What clue is in this entry?

2. How do you think it got there?

3. How is it related to the haunted hound?

Clue Keeper Entry 7

"What is all the yelling about?" Sally Warnicke came down the stairs. She was barefoot, wore a bathrobe, and carried a candelabra full of candles. "I've been afraid to come out of the tower with all the yelling and howling."

"Just what we needed!" I said, reaching for the candles.

"What in the world did you do to Uncle Neil's wall?" Sally asked, peering into the secret passage.

"If you'll lend us your candles, we'll take a look. Seems like there's a dog on the loose in the house," I said.

Sally handed me the brass candelabra. It looked a lot like the one that I'd lit earlier in the library. I noticed it even had a chip at the base like the other one. It had to be the same candelabra. But Sally had come down the stairs leading to the tower — not up the stairs from the first floor. I noticed Velma looking at her closely, too.

Sally's robe opened and I noticed she was still wearing jeans and a T-shirt underneath. She quickly pulled her robe tighter. "Let me get a flashlight from my room," she said.

"Guys, I think it's time to set a trap for a giant-size terrier," Velma said as she watched Sally run up the steps.

Velma's Mystery-Solving Tips

"I hope you found the 's on page 45. These are important clues. Answer the following questions."

1. What were the clues?

2. How do you think Sally got the candelabra out of the library when she said she'd been in her room all evening?

3. What could the gang tell from the fact that Sally still wore her clothing?

Clue Keeper Entry 8

"I think I know who's behind the giant dog," said Velma, "but I want to be sure. We're going to need Shaggy and Scooby to make my plan work."

"*Ro ray,*" Scooby said from the other side of the door.

"Not even for a Scooby Snack?" Velma asked.

"*Ruh-ruh,*" Scooby answered.

"How about three Scooby Snacks?" she asked.

The door flew open and Scooby came out — followed by Shaggy.

We discussed our plan, then I lit the candles and handed the candelabra to Shaggy. "I don't think I like this," Shaggy said.

"Don't worry," I told him. "We'll be there when you need us."

We sent Shaggy and Scooby into the passage and slid the panel shut behind them. Then we hurried to the library.

Velma went to the plaster flower that controlled the opening in the library and we waited.

I heard the click, click, click of the dog's nails first, then I heard him growl.

"Nice doggy, nice doggy," said Shaggy.

The growl grew louder.

I nodded to Velma and she pressed the flower. The wall opened and Daphne threw a net over the giant Jack Russell terrier poised over Shaggy and Scooby.

Ms. Jaffe rushed into the room. "I heard the dog!" she said.

"And would you like to see exactly who the dog is?" I asked her as Daphne lifted the net.

I reached in and snatched the dog's head off the huge terrier.

"So, what did you think of the mystery?" Fred asks.

You nod, still trying to sort out the suspects and clues.

"Do you think you know what happened?" asks Velma.

You pause, then nod again, slowly. You wish you were a little more sure.

"Maybe we can help. First think about which suspects had a reason to want people out of the house," says Daphne.

"Then, who could have been responsible for the clues we found," Fred says.

"Finally, who had the chance to be the haunted hound?" asks Daphne.

"A good way to come up with an answer is to count out any of the suspects who didn't have a motive to be the hound, who couldn't have had the means to leave the clues, or who didn't have an opportunity," Velma suggests.

"But, like, don't you want a hot dog first?" asks Shaggy, looking at the plate the waitress left you.

You aren't really that hungry. You scoot it over to Shaggy.

"Like, thanks."

Scooby looks at you, hurt. You motion to the waitress, and she brings you another plate. You give that one to Scooby. *"Rank rou!"* he says before stuffing the hot dog into his mouth in one bite. Those regular hot dogs aren't quite enough for these hungry boys.

"Take a few minutes, then we'll tell you what happened at the Haunted Hound," says Fred.

52

It's time for you to guess whodunnit! Do you think you know who it is? When you're ready, turn the page and discover the ending of <u>The Case of the Haunted Hound.</u>

"**T**he villain was Sally Warnicke," says Fred, "who wanted to get everyone out of the house so she could find the treasure she thought her uncle hid there."

"No one has found a treasure yet," Daphne adds, "but who knows?"

"Our first clue was the shiny powder we found on the floor in the library with a footprint in the middle of it," says Velma.

"That told us it wasn't really a giant hound haunting the Bed and Breakfast. It was a person," Fred puts in.

"Trent Kendall never had on shoes the entire evening and later, we saw Sally was barefoot," Velma adds. "Ms. Shaw wore shoes the whole time, so we knew she wasn't the one."

"We also knew the powder glowed just like the dog's eyes and teeth," Daphne explains.

"We figured it was rubbed around the eyes and the teeth of the dog mask to make them glow," Velma says.

"Then, I found some of the same powder on Fred's shirt. He remembered that Trent Kendall pulled him away from the bookshelf in the library, and Sally had pushed him away when he tried to help her with her suitcase — the one with the dog costume in it," Daphne tells you.

"Finally, Sally had the candelabra from the library, even though she came from the tower and we never saw her downstairs." Fred says.

Velma sits forward. "She must have moved back and forth through the secret passage," she says. "But the real clincher was when Fred and I noticed Sally was wearing clothes under her robe. She hadn't gone to bed early at all!"

"So, how did you do?" Fred asks.

"Remember," he says. "We've been doing this a long time and it took us a while to catch on to how mystery solving works. If you didn't get it this time, you will the next."

The waitress brings over another hot dog, covered with chili this time, and sets it in front of you.

You shake your head and she reaches for it.

"Wait!" says Shaggy. "If you don't want that . . ."

Before he can finish, you push the plate across the table.

"*Rooby-Rooby-Roo!*" says Scooby, licking his lips.